W9-BGY-096

Squiggz Rides the Big Storm

A Story about Overcoming Fear

Concept by Bruce Barry
Written by Sharon E. Lamson
Created and Illustrated by Wacky World Studios

zonderkidz

zonder**kidz**
The children's group of Zondervan

www.zonderkidz.com

Squiggz Rides the Big Storm
ISBN: 0-310-71005-7

Concept by Bruce Barry
Written by Sharon E. Lamson
Created and Illustrated by Wacky World Studios, LLC

Requests for information should be addressed to:
Zonderkidz, Grand Rapids, Michigan 49530

Editor: Amy DeVries
Art Direction: Bruce Barry and Brandt Elling Peters
Art Direction & Interior Design: Merit Alderink

Printed in China
06 07 08 09/CTC/4 3 2 1

For more Wacky World Studios information visit: www.wackyworld.tv

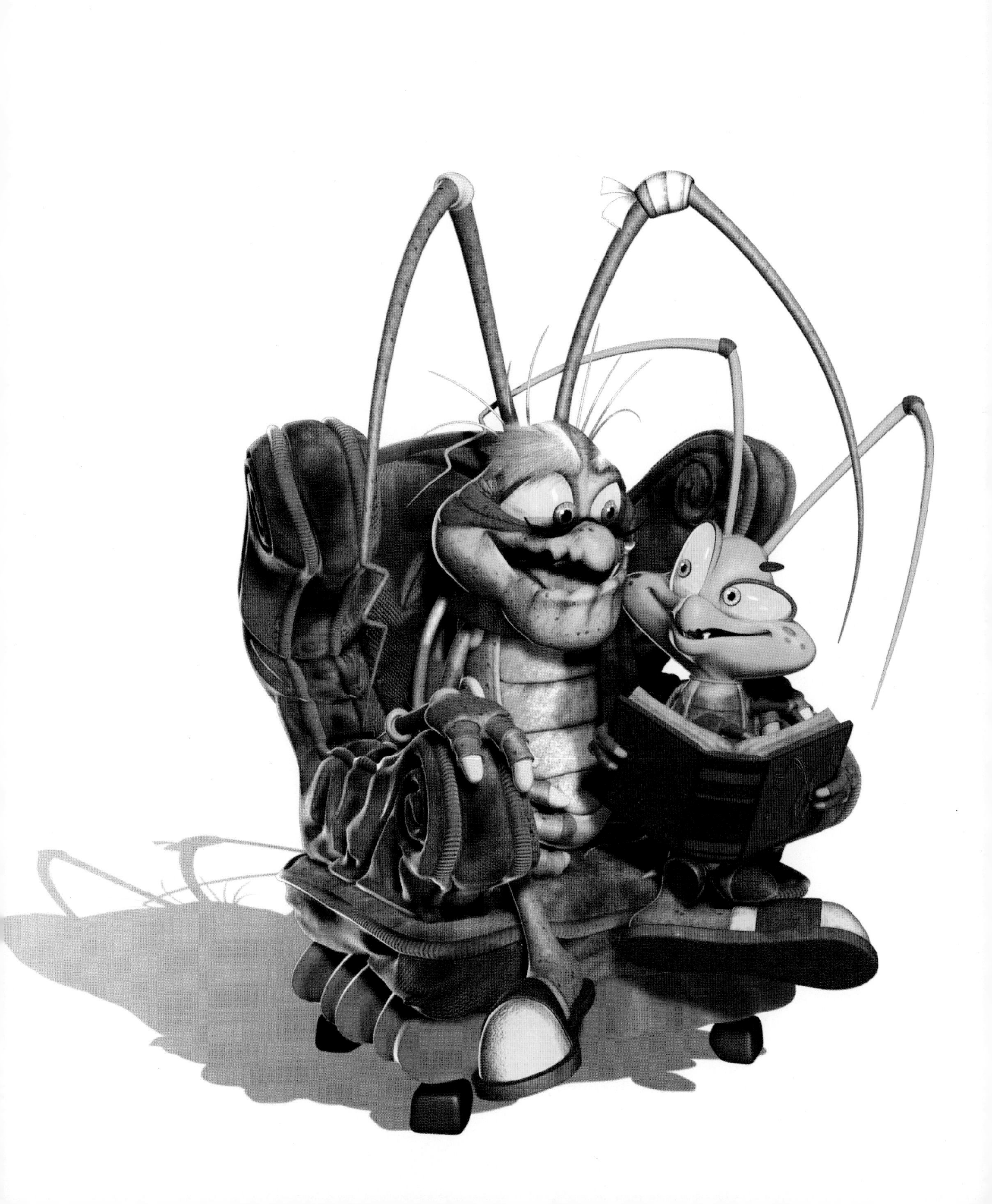

Squiggz raced into Nana's kitchen. "The people have closed the pier!" he yelled. "A hurricane is coming!"

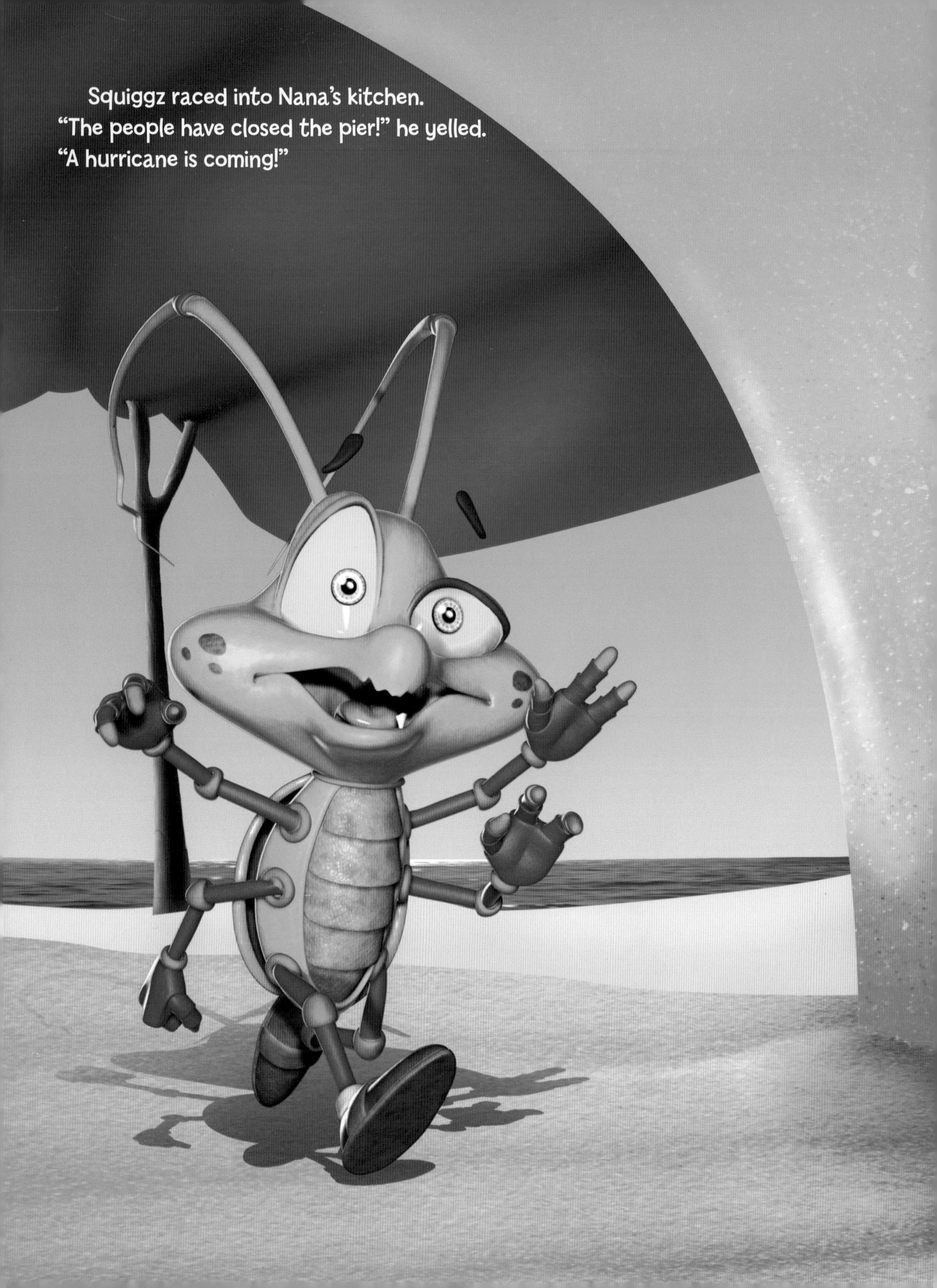

Nana checked her chocolate corn-chip cookies.

"We'll need food," she said. "I hope I've baked enough to last us."

Squiggz looked at the cookies. "Nana, you've baked enough to feed all the roaches in the world!"

Squiggz grabbed his Roach Ranger handbook.
"Nana, we have to move to higher ground. Fast!"

Grandpa Lou stepped into the room. "What's all the commotion?" he asked.
"A hurricane is coming!" cried Squiggz.
"Calm down, Squiggz," Grandpa Lou said. "Let's go see what's going on."

Outside, they saw Cosmo and Flutter scurry toward them.
"This is going to be a bad storm," Nana said. "I can feel it in my antennae."

Cosmo flipped through the pages of the Roach Ranger handbook. “There’s nothing in here about hurricanes,” he said. “But I know a Roach Ranger should always be prepared.”

Flutter paced back and forth. "How can we prepare? The pier will probably collapse. The storm will last forever. The ocean will wash us away. I'll never get my Junk Pile merit badge."

Flutter's wings beat faster and faster.

"I can see why you're named Flutter," said Squiggz. "The more you worry, the faster your wings fly."

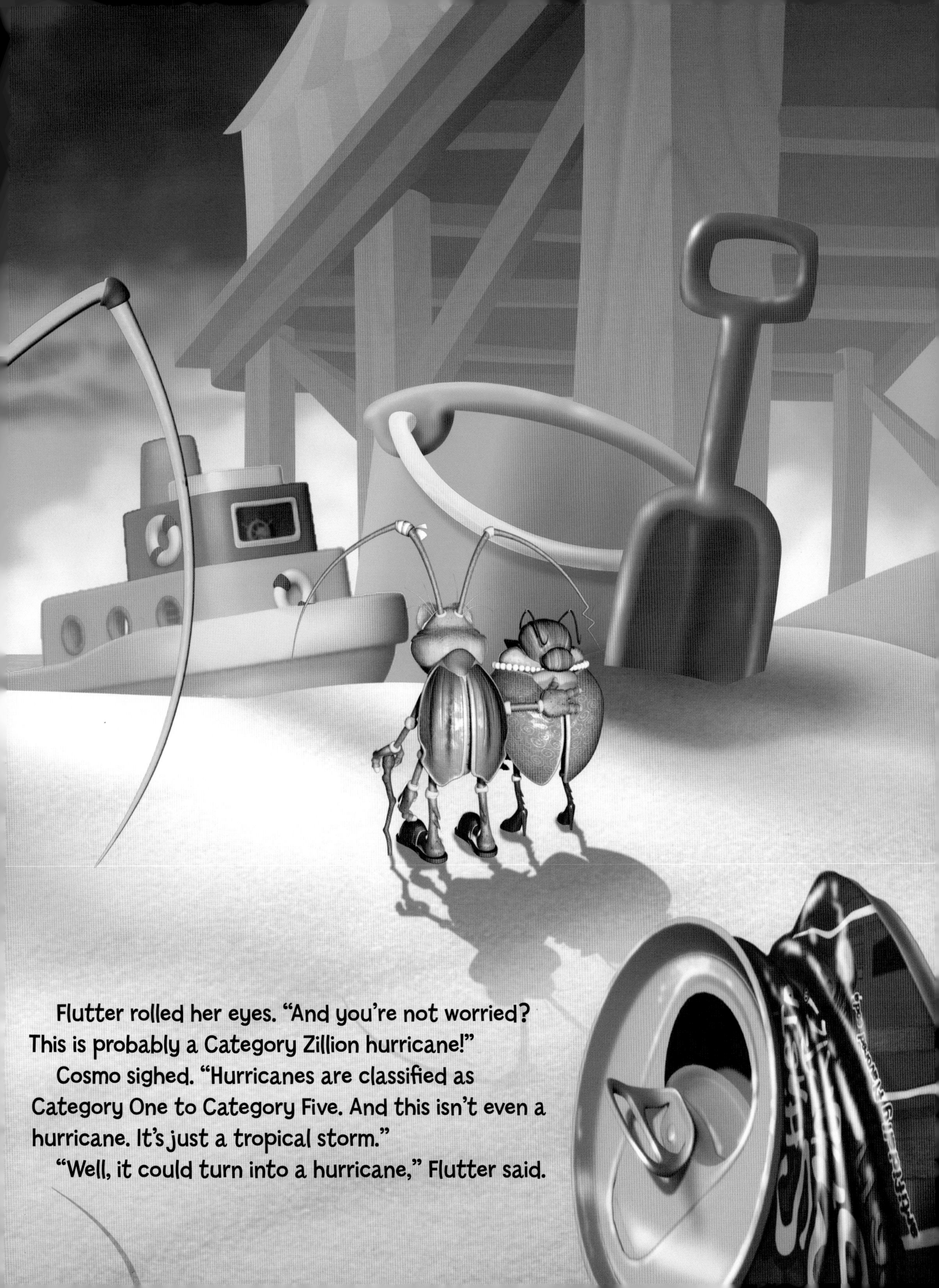

Flutter rolled her eyes. "And you're not worried? This is probably a Category Zillion hurricane!"

Cosmo sighed. "Hurricanes are classified as Category One to Category Five. And this isn't even a hurricane. It's just a tropical storm."

"Well, it could turn into a hurricane," Flutter said.

"How can you *not* be worried?" Flutter asked. "This isn't just a spring shower."

Squiggz pulled out his Bible. "Grandpa Lou told me that the Bible says we're not supposed to worry about stuff. Instead, we're supposed to ask God to take care of what's bothering us. Then his peace will help us not to be afraid."

"That's it? You just pray and then you don't care?" Flutter shook her head. "I don't get it."

"I believe God hears our prayers," Squiggz said. "He'll show us the way. Worrying won't help."

Just then Squiggz heard a *plip! plip!* Raindrops began falling. *Plip-plip-plip!* Faster and faster. Harder and harder.

"It's here! The hurricane of the century is here!" yelled Flutter. "What are we going to do?"

The wind whipped through their wings. The ocean's waves crashed onto the shore. Water washed over the pier.

"Hey, everybody!" he yelled. "Let's get into the boat!" Grandpa Lou and Nana scurried to the lower deck. Squiggz, Cosmo, and Flutter scrambled to the top deck.

Nana yelled out, "Try to keep your backpacks dry."

Flutter clutched her backpack and tried to keep her wings from fluttering.

Cosmo zipped his books into his backpack. He stared at the rising water.

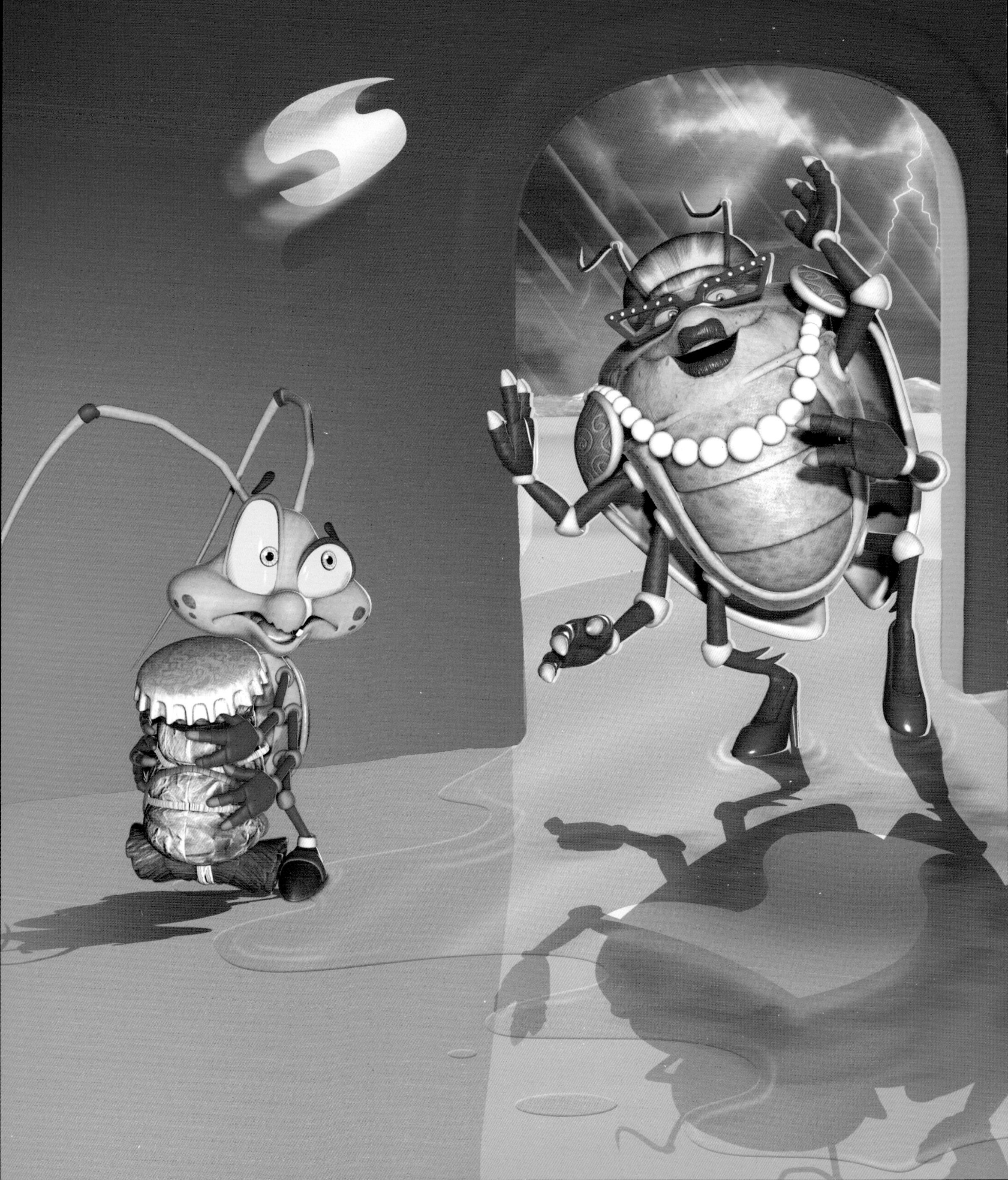

"I wonder if this is how Noah felt?" cried Nana. "Do you think we'll be in here forty days and forty nights? If we are, we're going to be very, very hungry."

Squiggz and his friends scooted to the lower deck. Squiggz said, "Grandpa Lou, will you show us where in the Bible it says not to worry about stuff?"

Grandpa Lou opened the Bible to Philippians 4 verses 6 and 7. "Don't worry about anything. Instead, tell God about everything. Ask and pray. Give thanks to him. Then God's peace will watch over your hearts and your minds because you belong to Christ Jesus."

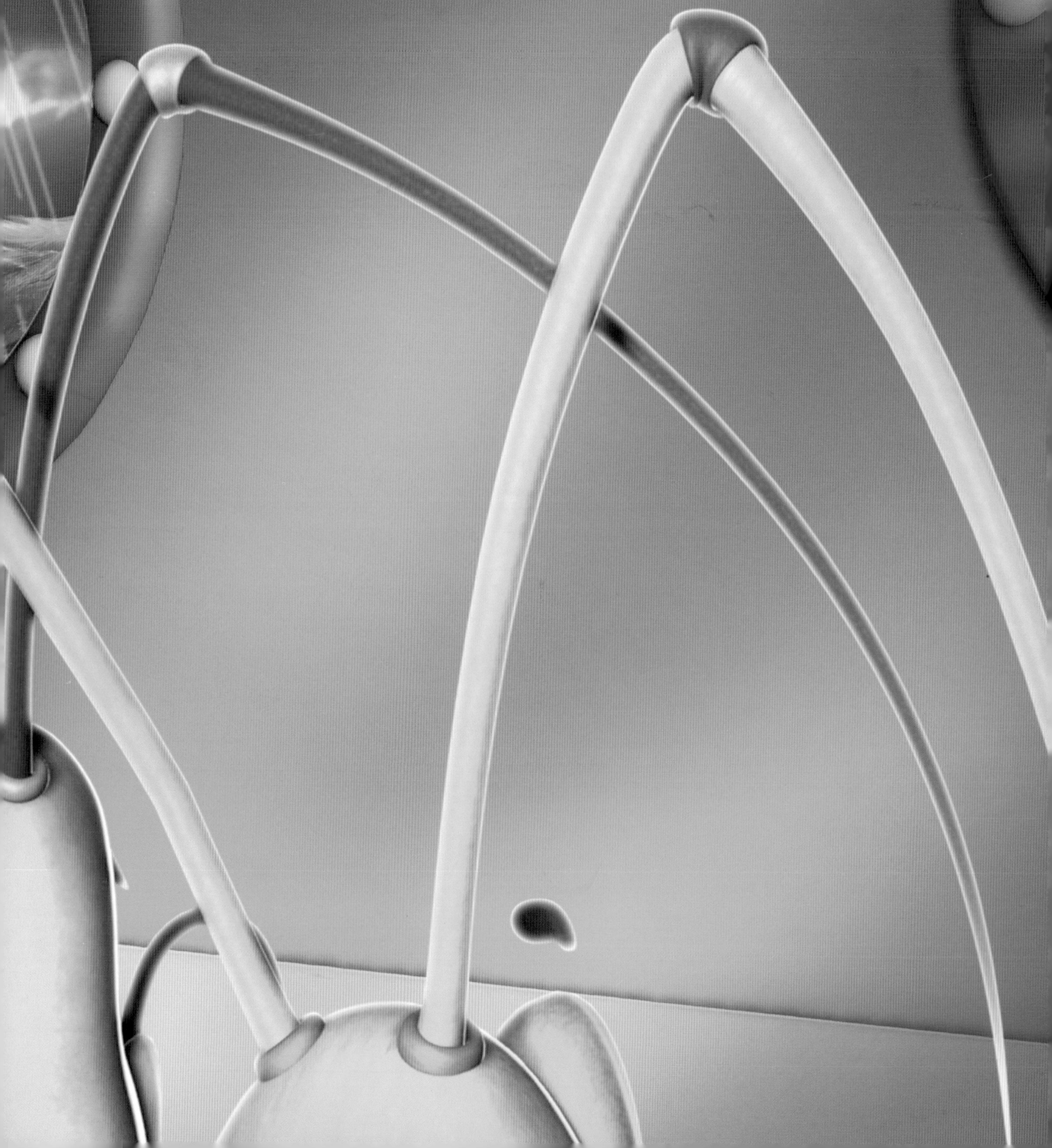

HOLY

Squiggz prayed, “Please God, take care of us. Help us to not worry about the storm. Help us to trust you. Amen.”

“Amen,” said Flutter and Cosmo.

Squiggz curled up against Grandpa Lou. Cosmo and Flutter huddled next to Nana. The wind howled. Waves roared. The tugboat rocked back and forth. Soon, everyone fell asleep.

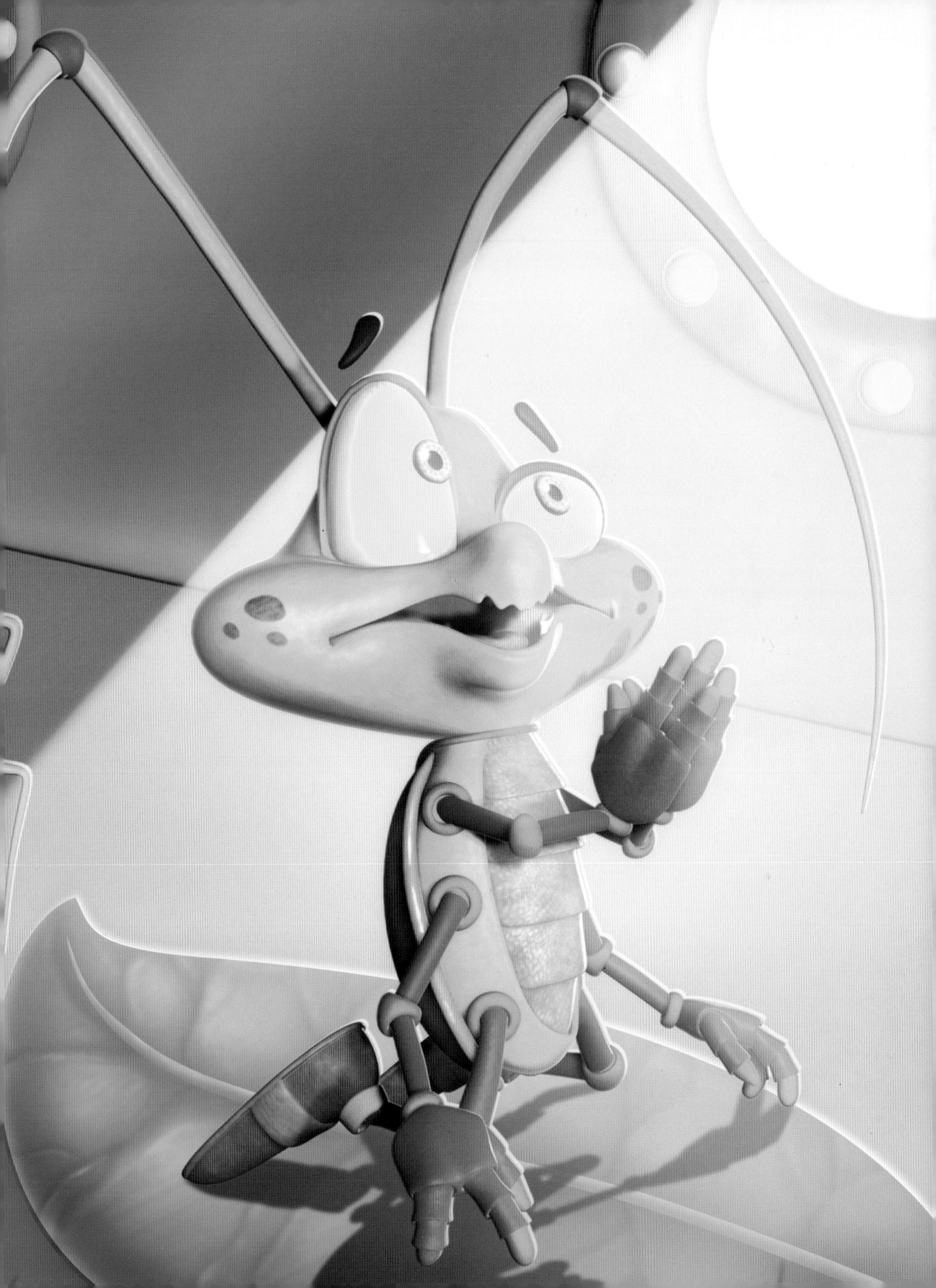

The next day, they scrambled outside. Gentle waves and the sounds of seagulls greeted them. They looked around. Panic Pier was still there. Storeowners took down the boards that had covered their shops' windows.

Squiggz, Cosmo, and Flutter made roach angels in the sand.

"You know," Squiggz said, "after I prayed, I really did feel peaceful."

Flutter danced around in the sand. "I prayed, too. And my wings stopped fluttering!"

"Awesome, Flutter!" said Squiggz.

"So we really don't have to worry," said Cosmo.

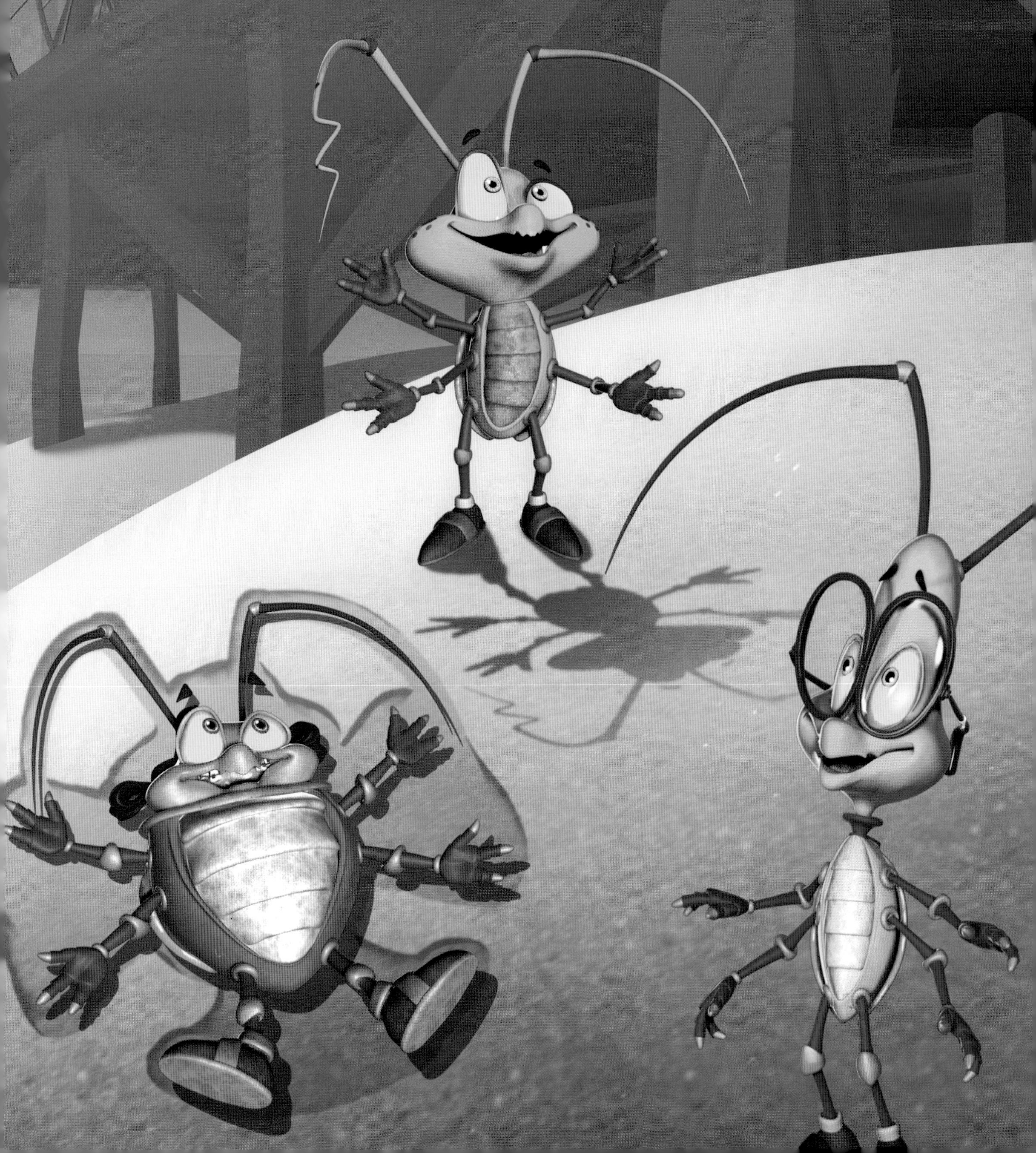